Jason Goes
to
Show-and-Tell

Text copyright © 1992 by Colleen Sutherland
Illustrations copyright © 1992 by Linda Weller
All rights reserved
Published by Bell Books
Boyds Mills Press, Inc.
A Highlights Company
910 Church Street
Honesdale, Pennsylvania 18431
Publisher Cataloging-in-Publication Data
Sutherland, Colleen.
Jason goes to show and tell / by Colleen Sutherland; illustrated
by Linda Weller.
[32]p. : col. ill. ;   cm.
Summary: Trying to remember everything to take to kindergarten on a cold and
snowy day, especially when teddy bear is coming along, involves repeated trips back
to the house for just one more thing.
ISBN 1-878093-89-4
1. Teddy bears—Fiction—Juvenile literature. [1. Teddy bears—Fiction.]
I. Weller, Linda, ill. II. Title.
                              [E]   1992
Library of Congress Catalog Card Number: 91-77613

First edition, 1992
Book designed by Tim Gillner.
The text of this book is set in 14-point Galliard.
The illustrations are watercolors.

Distributed by St. Martin's Press
Printed in Hong Kong

10 9 8 7 6 5 4 3 2 1

Jason Goes to Show-and-Tell

by Colleen Sutherland

Illustrated by Linda Weller

BELL BOOKS
BOYDS MILLS PRESS

To Chris, whose toleration makes it all possible

— C. S.

With love and thanks to Mom and Dad

— L. W.

Jason loved his teddy bear. He wanted to take it to kindergarten for show-and-tell. He hurried.

He opened the front door and ran outside. He tumbled into a snowbank.

"Oh, no!" Jason said. "My new school shoes will get wet." Jason ran back inside.

He searched high . . .   and he searched low . . .

until he found his boots in the bathtub.

He put on his boots and ran outside, into the snow.

There was a cold wind blowing. "Oh, my," Jason sighed. "My arms are freezing." He jumped back through the doorway.

He took off his boots (so he would not get the floor wet) and he searched high . . .

and he searched low until he found his orange jacket—under the kitchen table.

"Hurry, Jason," his mommy called.
       He put on his jacket
              and he put on his boots
and he started off for kindergarten with his teddy bear for show-and-tell.

He had taken only a few steps when the wind began tangling the curls on his head. "Oh, no!" Jason ran back home.

He took off his jacket
     and he took off his boots (so he would not get the floor wet)

and he searched high . . .

and he searched low . . .

until he found his red knitted hat — behind the TV.

He put on his hat
and he put on his jacket
and he put on his boots
and he started off once again for kindergarten with his teddy bear for
show-and-tell.

"Brrrrrr!" Jason's teeth chattered as he came to the fire hydrant. The wind whirled around his head. "My neck is SOOOO COLD!" He rushed home and ran right into his mommy's arms.

She smiled. "Did you forget your scarf, Jason?"
    Jason took off his hat
        and he took off his jacket
            and he took off his boots (so he would not get the floor wet)

and he searched high . . .   and he searched low . . .

until he found his green scarf — on top of the refrigerator.

Then Jason put on his scarf
and he put on his hat
and he put on his jacket
and he put on his boots
and he walked off to kindergarten with his teddy bear for show-and-tell.

Halfway down the street, Jason began to cry. "My fingers are turning blue." The school bus driver saw Jason's tears. She rubbed his fingers to make them warm. Then she drove him back to his house to get his mittens.

"What did you forget, Jason?" his mommy asked.
Jason took off his scarf
      and he took off his hat
            and he took off his jacket
                  and he took off his boots (so he would not get the floor wet)

and he searched high . . .   and he searched low for his purple mittens.

Jason could not find his mittens anywhere! He sobbed, because he would miss show-and-tell. Jason's mommy hugged him. "Where did you leave your mittens last?" she asked.

Jason and his mommy searched high . . . and they searched low until they found the purple mittens — on his bed. Jason promised his mommy that he would put his things away when he came home from kindergarten.

Then he put on his scarf
and he put on his hat
and he put on his jacket
and he put on his boots
and he put on his mittens
and off he went with his mommy for show-and-tell.

When Jason got to kindergarten, he kissed his mommy good-bye.
Then he took off his mittens
and he took off his scarf
and he took off his hat
and he took off his jacket
and he took off his boots (so he would not get the floor wet)
and he put everything away carefully.

He sat down next to Gordon. Then he remembered.
"Oh, no! I forgot my teddy bear!"